Dedicated to the inspiration for all that I do in life...my precious daughter, Ella.

- Kara Haas

www.mascotbooks.com

For more information, please contact:
Mascot Books
560 Herndon Parkway #120
Herndon, VA 20170
info@mascotbooks.com

CPSIA Code: PRT0912A
Library of Congress Control Number: 2012936267
ISBN: 1-620860-33-3
ISBN-13: 978-1-620860-33-5

Printed in the United States

Will You Be My Flower Girl?

Kara Haas

illustrated by
Kate Themel

A Special Note to the Reader

This book is for every little girl out there who wasn't sure of what a flower girl was; and for every bride who wanted their special flower girl to experience the magic of the day.

- Kara Haas

Kate the Great, who was almost eight, was the best daydreamer known this side of Mississippi State. She knew today was sure to be full of adventure. Kate was expecting a visit from her favorite aunt, Sara. Aunt Sara showed up driving a grasshopper! Well, the old green car certainly looked like a grasshopper to Kate!

"Hi, my favorite little girl!" Aunt Sara said as she lifted Kate up.

"I am a porcupine today, Aunt Sara, so watch out for my prickly quills," smiled Kate.

"I have something important to talk to you about today, Miss Porcupine," Aunt Sara said to Kate.

"Will it make me the Princess of Porcupines, Aunt Sara?"

Aunt Sara laughed her jolly laugh, "No, but I think it will make you very happy! Will you be my flower girl?" asked Aunt Sara. Kate gave Aunt Sara a very puzzled look.

A flour girl didn't sound like fun to Kate. She frowned,
"I do not like flour. Flour is itchy, and it tastes like dirt!"

Aunt Sara laughed and smiled kindly at Kate. "Since when have you become a dirt eater, Kate?" Kate scowled at Aunt Sara and folded her arms crossly. "Come for a walk with me, Kate. I will tell you what a flower girl is." But Kate did not hear Aunt Sara. She had already started to daydream...

AAA-CCHHHOOOO! AAA-CCHHHOOOO! Kate found
herself sneezing! She was inside a giant jar full of
flour. Kate was poured out along with the white,
powdery flour down a long, plastic spout...

POOF! Kate found herself inside a mixing bowl. OUCH! A huge plastic spoon kept tapping Kate on the side of her head.

SPLOOSH! A landslide of eggs came splashing down on Kate's head. WOOAAHH! Kate found herself in a whirlpool of water, eggs, and flour.

BONK! BONK! Brown chocolate chips came raining down on Kate.

YUM! Kate gobbled up some of the chocolate chips. All of this mixing was making her very hungry!

Oh my goodness! What is all of this gooey stuff all over Kate's arms? It must be chocolate chip cookie dough! Kate was inside a bowl of chocolate chip cookie dough! Kate was a flour girl, and the baker mistakenly thought Kate was flour!

"I am not flour!" Kate shouted out loud, "I am a little girl!"

"Kate, Kate, it's okay," Aunt Sara said soothingly. "Where are you now, my favorite little daydreamer?"

"Oh, Aunt Sara! Please rescue me from the baker!" Kate yelled as she jumped into Aunt Sara's arms. "The baker thinks that I am a flour girl!"

Aunt Sara stroked Kate's blond hair. "Kate, you must have been having a 'daymare' - a daytime nightmare!"

Aunt Sara took Kate for a walk. She held Kate's hand as she explained what a flower girl does. "This kind of flower girl has nothing to do with white baking powder."

Aunt Sara explained to Kate that she was getting married, and she wanted Kate to be a special part of her wedding day. A flower girl is a very special part of the day and participates in the ceremony.

Aunt Sara told Kate that a flower girl is the name for the girl in the wedding who carries the basket of flowers. The flower girl wears a pretty white dress, new white shoes, and gets a fancy hair-do! The flower girl walks down the aisle before the bride, Aunt Sara, and gently throws flower petals down while she walks. That way Aunt Sara can walk on beautiful flower petals. The flower girl then stands next to the bride during the wedding ceremony - a very grown up job!

When Aunt Sara was done explaining, Kate smiled. "I will not be thrown into chocolate chip batter or mistaken for flour?"

Aunt Sara laughed, "Oh, Kate, you have such a wonderful imagination! Only good and happy things happen when you are a flower girl. It is a very special job for very special little girls!"

"I want to be your flower girl, Aunt Sara!" Kate shouted happily. This made Aunt Sara so happy.

When the wedding day came, Kate couldn't be happier. Kate wore the most beautiful white dress ever worn by anybody! It had white satin, bows, and puffy white stuff that looked magical! Kate's new white shoes were sparkly and made a CLICK-CLICK sound when she walked. Kate's Mom had curled her hair so that it went BOUNCE-BOUNCE, like a pogo stick.

Kate carried a white wicker basket with beautiful pink flower petals. The wicker basket felt a little bit heavy for only containing flower petals. Hmmm... Kate looked down at her basket. There, hidden underneath the flower petals, was a giant chocolate chip cookie! Kate giggled and looked back at Aunt Sara, all dressed in her beautiful wedding dress. Aunt Sara winked and Kate knew she was going to enjoy being a flour - whoops - flower girl!

The End

About the Author

I wrote this book as I was contemplating my own wedding and reflecting upon my own experience as a flower girl. When I was a flower girl I was so nervous and unsure of my role. I wanted to use this story to explain the unique role of a flower girl to the special little girls in my own wedding. Since conquering flower girl I have assumed many other roles in my life including: marathon runner, teacher, writer, wife, and, most recently, mom. It is my role as a mom that I treasure most. I cherish all the evenings spent reading stories to my daughter. I hope moms and brides everywhere will treasure reading this book to their little girl.